Little Miss Muffet

Retold by Russell Punter

Illustrated by Lorena Alvarez

Reading consultant: Alison Kelly
Roehampton University

Little Miss Muffet,
sat on a tuffet,

eating her curds
and whey.

Along came a
spider,

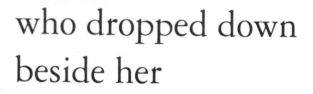

who dropped down
beside her

and frightened Miss
Muffet away.

"Help!" cried
Miss Muffet.

She ran from her tuffet

and into the woods
down below.

"Come back!" called
the spider.

He rushed off
to find her.

"I'm sorry for scaring you so."

The little girl sighed.

"What a bad place to hide."

"Now I'm lost! I'll be stuck here all night."

Then she heard
a deep growl

grrrrrr!

and an ear-splitting
howl.

OWWWWOOOOO!

They gave poor Miss
Muffet a fright.

13

A big wolf jumped out.
He said with a shout,

"It's time for my dinner, my dear."

"I'll have little girl pie!"

"Put her down!" came
a cry.

"Don't worry —
Seb Spider is here."

The wolf gave a smile.
"I do like your style.

But what can you do
against me?"

"I'll show you," said Seb.

He spun a strong web

and tied the bad wolf
to a tree.

21

Miss Muffet said, "Seb, what a wonderful web.

Now let's go!"

So Seb showed
her the way.

Now she's friends with
Seb Spider.

He hangs down
beside her

and spins for Miss
Muffet all day.

PUZZLES

Puzzle 1

Can you spot the differences between these two pictures? There are six to find.

Puzzle 2
Find these things in
the picture:

spider   book   tree

web   girl   bird

Puzzle 3
Choose the best speech bubble for each picture.

Answers to puzzles

Puzzle 1

Puzzle 2

tree   spider   web

web

girl   book   bird

Puzzle 3

Put her down!

Come back!

About the rhyme

The original version of *Little Miss Muffet* first appeared in print over two hundred years ago.

Curd is thickened milk used to make cheese. Whey is a watery liquid made when the milk is thickened.

Series editor: Lesley Sims

First published in 2012 by Usborne Publishing Ltd., Usborne House, 83-85 Saffron Hill, London EC1N 8RT, England. www.usborne.com
Copyright © 2012 Usborne Publishing Ltd.